D1254541

PIGEON, PIGEON

by Caron Lee Cohen
pictures by G. Brian Karas

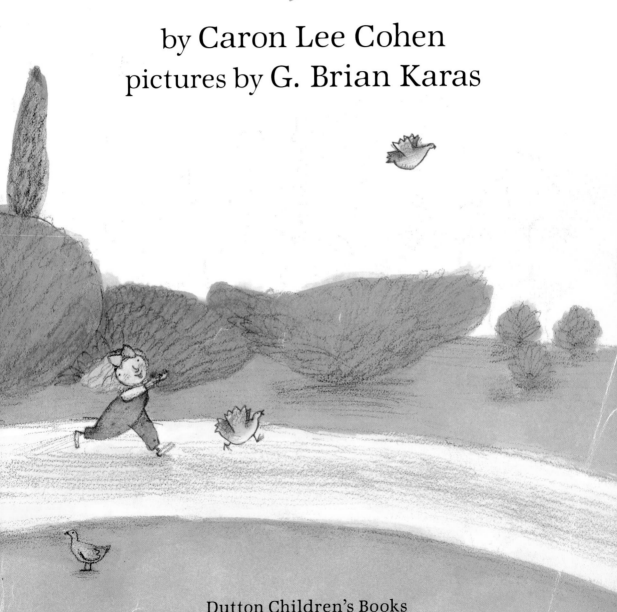

Dutton Children's Books
NEW YORK

Published in the United States by
Dutton Children's Books,
a division of Penguin Books USA Inc.
375 Hudson Street, New York, New York 10014

Designer: Joseph Rutt

Printed in Hong Kong by South China Printing Co.

First Edition   10 9 8 7 6 5 4 3 2 1

Library of Congress Cataloging-in-Publication Data

Cohen, Caron Lee.
   Pigeon, pigeon / by Caron Lee Cohen; pictures
by G. Brian Karas. —1st ed.
      p.   cm.
   Summary: A child and her parents find
different animals to view at the zoo.
   ISBN 0-525-44866-7
   [1. Zoo animals—Fiction.   2. Zoos—Fiction.
   3. Perception—Fiction.]   I. Karas, G. Brian, ill.
   II. Title.
PZ7.C65974Pi 1992   91-36177 CIP   AC

To Mommy, Daddy, Elaine
—C.L.C.

To Marissa and Michele
—G.B.K.

"Lion, lion!"

"Pigeon, pigeon!"

"Look! A hippopotamus."

"Look! Spider."

"Come, zebra."

"Come, caterpillar."

"Watch the chimp climb."

"Up, up, squirrel."

"Look at the parrots fly."

"Oooo, flies."

"Scary crocodile!"

"Scary!"

"What big teeth!"

"Big teeth!"

"Ooo! Prairie dogs."

"Ooo! Hot dogs."

"Look! A bear."

"Nice bear."

"Where did it go?"

"Listen! How loud!"

"Too loud."

"Touch the elephant's trunk."

"No!"

"Bye-bye, zoo."

"Bye-bye, zoo."